When Dogs Dream

By Jean Ekman Adams

Rio CHiCo
BOOKS FOR CHILDREN

Rio Chico, an imprint of Rio Nuevo Publishers®
P. O. Box 5250, Tucson, AZ 85703-0250
(520) 623-9558, www.rionuevo.com

Editorial: Theresa Howell
Book design: David Jenney

Printed in China.

6   5   4   3   2   1   13   14   15   16   17   18

Library of Congress Cataloging-in-Publication Data

Adams, Jean Ekman, 1942-
  When dogs dream / words and pictures by Jean Ekman Adams.
      p. cm.
  Summary: Reveals some of the secret dreams of stray dogs in the desert Southwest, such as learning to drive a car, planning parties, or just wearing a collar that jingles. Includes a list of rescue groups that help these dogs.
  ISBN 978-1-933855-84-4 (hardcover : alk. paper)
  [1. Dogs—Fiction. 2. Pet adoption—Fiction.] I. Title.
  PZ7.A2163If 2013
  [E]—dc23
                            2012035921

For Jill and Cindy

We are four desert
dogs—Snarfy, Darryl,
Shine, and Shorty.
 We live out under the
great Western sky.

When it rains, we drink puddles.

When it snows, we huddle.

We are nice and dirty. We don't belong to anyone.

But yet, sometimes we dream.

What would it be like to wear collars and tags and live inside? Would we jingle?

Would we sit at the table?

Could we drive the car?

Could we go to school and learn to read?

Maybe we could learn to cook—

and give little parties.

When it freezes, we could sleep in the bed.

And when it thunders, we could sleep under it.

We would love to go on vacation,

fly in the nice part of the plane,

and swim in the ocean.

Shorty would like to go to the beauty parlor.

And the rest of us would like to chase something.

But no dog wants to play golf,

or do the ironing.

Shorty wishes she were taller;   Darryl, smarter;

Snarfy, cleaner;

and Shine, braver.

We all wish we had a home.

Something small and cozy. Nothing fancy.

We can pound,

and patch,

and paint,

and pump.

And we can make
our dreams come true.

SHORTY
SNARFY
DARRYL
SHINE

How You Can Help

Shorty, Snarfy, Darryl, and Shine were lucky, but many southwestern strays are homeless. These dogs are appreciative, intelligent, and sensitive. I know. I have one.

The rescue groups below go above and beyond in helping needy dogs. Contact any of them to adopt, sponsor, or donate. Or look into shelters close to where you live.

Blackhat Humane Society
Durango, Colorado

Rezdog Rescue
Gallup, New Mexico

For Pets' Sake Humane Society
Cortez, Colorado

Round Valley Animal Rescue
Eager, Arizona

Kayenta Animal Shelter
Kayenta, Arizona

Tenderfoot Rescue
Gallup, New Mexico

Noah's Ark Rescue
Glendale, Arizona

Tuba City Humane Society
Tuba City, Arizona

Pet Allies Animal Rescue
Show Low, Arizona

Thank you,
Jean, Shorty, Snarfy,
Darryl, and Shine

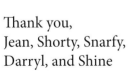